I WILL NOT READ THIS BOOK

by CECE MENG   Illustrated by JOY ANG

CLARION BOOKS

Houghton Mifflin Harcourt • Boston New York 2011

Clarion Books
215 Park Avenue South
New York, New York 10003

Clarion Books is an imprint of Houghton Mifflin Harcourt Publishing Company.

www.hmhbooks.com

The illustrations in this book were executed digitally.
The text was set in 21-point Futuramano Condenced Light.

Library of Congress Cataloging-in-Publication Data
Meng, Cece.
I will not read this book / written by Cece Meng ; illustrated by Joy Ang.
p. cm.
Summary: A child adamantly refuses to read a book, regardless of the increasingly outrageous circumstances that might occur.
ISBN 978-0-547-04971-7
[1. Books and reading—Fiction.] I. Ang, Joy, ill. II. Title.
PZ7.M5268Iae 2011
[E]—dc22
2010043175
Manufactured in China
LEO 10 9 8 7 6 5 4 3 2 1
4500294805

To Alex —C.M.

To Mom, Dad, and Josh for your constant support —J.A.

WAIT. Before I read this book,

I have to floss my teeth   and wash behind my ears   and feed my fish.

WAIT.

Before I read this book,

6

 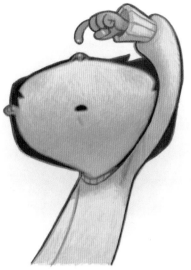 

I have to sip some water   and scratch the tip of my nose   and clean under my bed.

WAIT.

I changed my mind. I am not going to read today. Reading is hard and I don't read fast and sometimes there are words I don't know. I will not read this book and . . .

YOU CAN'T MAKE ME.

I will not read this book even if you hang me upside down . . .

by one toe.

I will not read this book
even if you hang me upside down
by one toe . . .

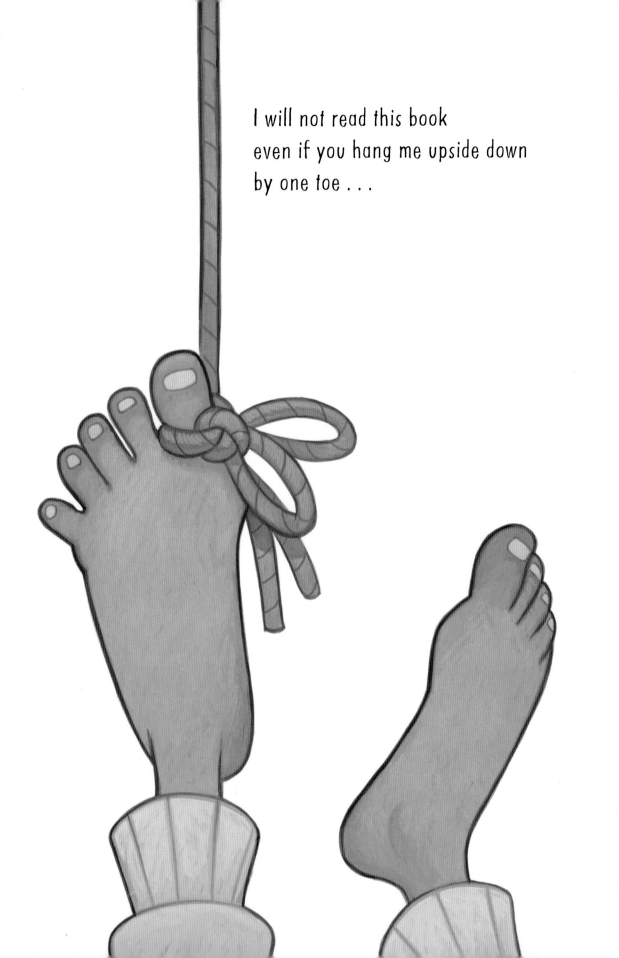

over a cliff.

I will not read this book
even if you hang me upside down
by one toe
over a cliff . . .

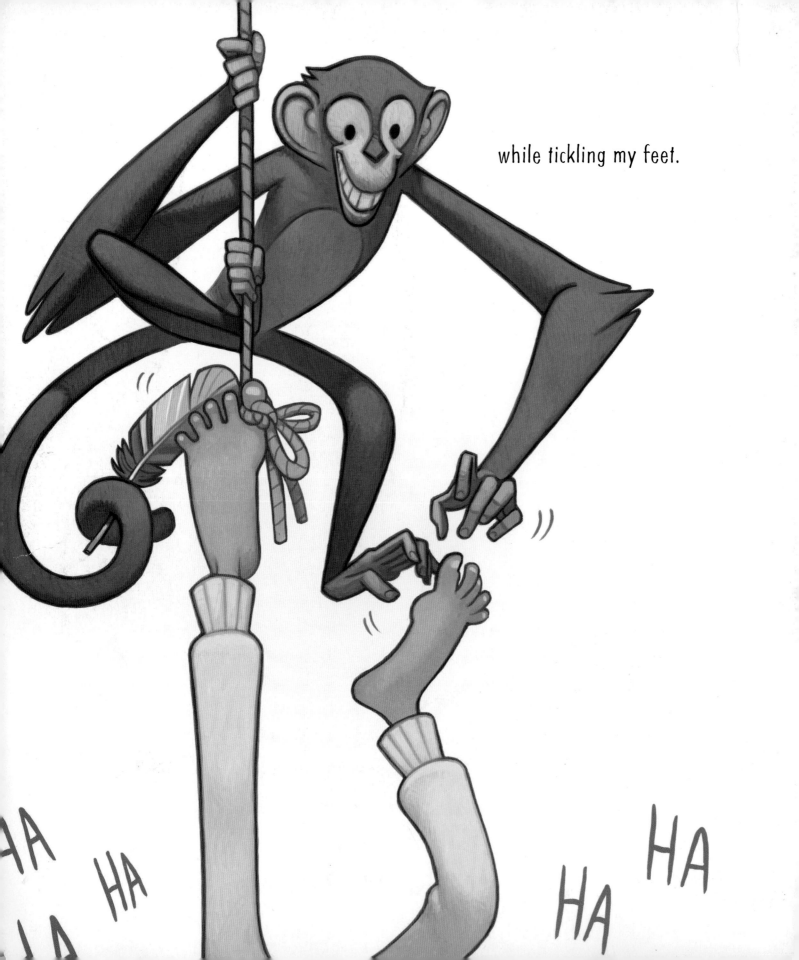

while tickling my feet.

I will not read this book
even if you hang me upside down
by one toe
over a cliff
while tickling my feet . . .

in a rainstorm.

I will not read this book
even if you hang me upside down
by one toe
over a cliff
while tickling my feet
in a rainstorm . . .

17

with lightning above.

I will not read this book

even if you hang me upside down

by one toe

over a cliff

while tickling my feet

in a rainstorm

with lightning above and . . .

sharks down below.

I will not read this book

even if you hang me upside down

by one toe

over a cliff

while tickling my feet

in a rainstorm

with lightning above

and sharks down below and . . .

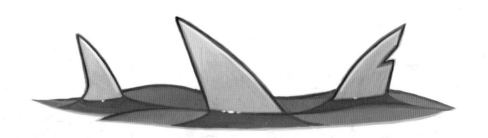

a dragon comes along
and blows smoke in my eyeballs.

I will not read this book
even if you hang me upside down
by one toe
over a cliff
while tickling my feet
in a rainstorm
with lightning above
and sharks down below
and a dragon comes along
and blows smoke in my eyeballs and . . .

all the while there's a
speeding train coming toward us.

I will not read this book

even if you hang me upside down

by one toe

over a cliff

while tickling my feet

in a rainstorm

with lightning above

and sharks down below

and a dragon comes along and

blows smoke in my eyeballs

and all the while there's a

speeding train coming toward us and . . .

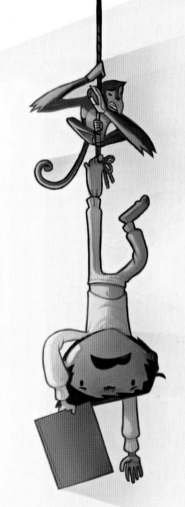

I have to sneeze.

I will not read this book

even if you hang me upside down

by one toe

over a cliff

while tickling my feet

in a rainstorm

with lightning above

and sharks down below

and a dragon comes along and

blows smoke in my eyeballs

and all the while there's a

speeding train coming toward us

and I sneeze and . . .

YOU DROP ME!

If you drop me, I might change my mind and read.

But only if you catch me.

Then I will read this book with you.